33052013238276

BY JAKE MADDOX

illustrated by Sean Tiffany

text by Bob Temple

Librarian Reviewer
Chris Kreie
Media Specialist, Eden Prairie Schools, MN
MS in Information Media, St. Cloud State University, MN

Reading Consultant
Mary Evenson
Middle School Teacher, Edina Public Schools, MN
MA in Education, University of Minnesota

STONE ARCH BOOKS
Minneapolis   San Diego

Jake Maddox Books are published by Stone Arch Books,
A Capstone Imprint
1710 Roe Crest Drive
North Mankato, Minnesota 56003
www.capstonepub.com

Library of Congress Cataloging-in-Publication Data
Maddox, Jake.
  Batter Up! / by Jake Maddox; illustrated by Sean Tiffany.
  p. cm. — (Impact Books — A Jake Maddox Sports Story)
  ISBN 978-1-4342-0465-3 (library binding)
  ISBN 978-1-4342-0515-5 (paperback)
  [1. Baseball—Fiction.] I. Tiffany, Sean, ill. II. Title.
PZ7.M25643Bat 2008
[Fic]—dc22   2007031257

Summary: Caleb has always batted with the same wood bat. But this
year, his new team's coach wants him to use an aluminum bat. When
his coach sees what Caleb can do with the wood bat, he agrees to let
him use it — until the other team accuses Caleb of tampering with the
bat! With his favorite bat out of commission, Caleb's forced to use the
aluminum bat. How is he supposed to help his team win when he keeps
striking out?

Art Director: Heather Kindseth
Graphic Designer: Kay Fraser

Printed in the United States of America in Stevens Point, Wisconsin.
032012
006660R

TABLE OF CONTENTS

Chapter 1

DECIDING THE GAME

Caleb was on deck, waiting for his turn at bat. He watched closely as Taylor stepped into the batter's box for their team.

Secretly, Caleb wished that Taylor would strike out. Caleb didn't want to lose, but he also didn't want to bat.

It was the bottom of the last inning. Two outs. Runners on first and second. The Spuds trailed 4–3, so the outcome of the game hung in the balance.

Taylor was not a strong hitter, so Caleb knew the chance was small that he'd get the hit to win the game.

If Taylor struck out, Caleb wouldn't have to bat. And Caleb really didn't want to have to bat.

The Oilers' pitcher wound up and delivered a pitch. Taylor didn't move.

"Strike one!" the umpire bellowed.

Caleb tried not to smile.

Standing on deck, Caleb wondered where his confidence had gone.

Only last summer, Caleb was one of the best hitters in the Dayton League. He had hit more home runs than anyone, and he had one of the league's best batting averages, too.

After all, that's why Coach Bergen asked him to try out for the Spuds.

The Spuds were a traveling team. They played against teams from other cities all around the area, and they competed for the District 9 Championship in the playoffs at the end of every season.

It was a much more intense league to play in than the Dayton League.

Now it was the first game of the season. The Spuds were playing against their biggest rivals, the Oilers, who were from a neighboring town.

It was a chance for the Spuds to start the season off on the right foot.

But for Caleb, it had started badly. In each of his first three times at bat, Caleb had struck out.

In fact, he hadn't even made contact with the ball.

"Strike two!" the umpire yelled. Taylor shook his head.

Caleb took a deep breath.

Caleb swung a bat back and forth. He stopped and eyed it. It was black and had a bright gold logo on the side.

All the other kids loved that bat, but Caleb didn't. Like all the bats the team used, it was aluminum.

But Caleb had his own bat, a wooden one, which he had used for three years.

To Caleb, the wood bat was like magic. He always came through with a hit in an important time of a game, as long as he had the wood bat.

In his old league, coach after coach had tried to get Caleb to use aluminum.

Every other kid in the league used an aluminum bat. But Caleb always stuck with his wood one, and no coach ever lived to regret letting him use it.

This year, playing for the Spuds, Caleb's coach had told him there was no way he could use the wood bat.

The pitcher stepped into his delivery. The runners edged off the bases. Taylor dug in. Caleb closed his eyes and waited for the thud of the catcher's glove.

When he heard it, he opened his eye. Taylor was bent over, holding his side. The thud had been the sound of Taylor getting hit by the pitch.

Caleb's shoulders sank.

Taylor shook off the pain and jogged down to first base. Each of the runners moved up a base. Now the bases were loaded.

Win or lose, Caleb would have to decide the game. With calls of "Come on, Caleb, you can do it!" all around him, Caleb turned around and walked slowly back into the dugout.

"Hey, Caleb!" Coach Bergen yelled from the third-base coach's box. "Where are you going?"

Caleb didn't answer. He silently walked back into the dugout. He unzipped the end of his equipment bag and pulled out his wood bat.

Chapter 2

THE MAGIC BAT

Without a word, Caleb walked out of the dugout and headed back toward the batter's box.

Coach Bergen yelled, "Time out!" The umpire gave the signal, and Coach Bergen trotted toward the batter's box.

Caleb sighed. He already knew exactly what was going to happen. There was no way Coach Bergen would be okay with him using the wood bat.

Caleb would be forced to use the aluminum bat. Then he would strike out and his team would lose.

The coach walked up to Caleb and put his arm around him.

"What's going on here, Caleb?" the coach asked. "You know how the league feels about kids using wood bats."

"Yes, I know," Caleb said. "But I don't like the aluminum ones and I've always felt great with this bat in my hands. Here. Hold it."

Caleb handed the bat to Coach Bergen.

"You're right, Caleb," the coach said. "It feels great."

The coach made a few practice swings with the wood bat. Then he handed it back to Caleb.

Coach Bergen sighed. He said, "The problem is, if you use this bat, they are only going to pitch you inside."

Caleb nodded. "I know. I'm used to that," he said.

The coach shook his head. "I know you are," he said.

He looked at Caleb for a moment. Then he continued, "With an aluminum bat, you can fight that pitch off and still hit it out of the infield. A wood bat might break, and then we'd be done."

Caleb could hear the murmurs of the players in the field.

"Is he really going to use a wood bat?" one of them said. "That's old school!"

Caleb looked Coach Bergen in the eye.

"Please, let me use it this one time," Caleb said. "If I don't get a hit, I'll put it away for the rest of the year. I promise. Just give me this one shot, Coach."

Coach Bergen thought for a second. Then he nodded. He turned and jogged back to the third-base coach's box.

A wide grin swept across Caleb's face.

Suddenly, it didn't matter that winning or losing the game was in his hands. It didn't matter that he had struck out three times. It didn't matter that this was his only chance to prove that his bat was usable.

All that mattered was that he had the chance.

Gently swinging his bat, Caleb stepped into the batter's box and eyed the Oilers' pitcher.

Caleb took his stance, and gently pushed the bat through the hitting zone with a few wide, slow sweeps.

As the pitcher went into his windup, Caleb's grip on the magic bat tightened.

The pitcher delivered. It was hard and fast, and cut in toward Caleb's belt.

He started to swing, but quickly stopped. The pitch almost hit him.

"Ball one!" the umpire called.

Caleb didn't move. He stared back at the pitcher, thinking about what might come next. He expected another inside pitch, and he got one.

Caleb timed his swing perfectly, and met the ball well out in front of home plate. He pulled it hard.

The ball shot down the third-base line, forcing Coach Bergen to duck out of the way.

"Whew!" the coach called. "Straighten that out, and we'll have a winner!"

The feeling of the ball cracking into his wood bat reminded Caleb how much he liked it.

By the time the next pitch was delivered, Caleb was smiling at the pitcher.

This time, the ball stayed over the middle of the plate.

Caleb didn't hesitate. He drove his back leg forward, turned his hips perfectly, and met the ball dead center.

Crack!

The ball sailed high out to left field.

The left fielder started to run back. Then he realized that he didn't have a chance of catching it.

As the ball landed on a hillside twenty feet beyond the fence, Caleb's teammates screamed and cheered.

Chapter 3

TAMPERED WITH?

As he rounded second base, Caleb could see the crowd that was forming for him around home plate.

Two of his teammates had already run over the plate. Another was quickly rounding third base.

The rest of the teammates were gathered behind home plate. They were jumping up and down and screaming. The people in the stands watching were cheering too.

By the time Caleb's foot hit third base, he felt like he was flying.

He had done it. Caleb had just won the first game of the season for his team. Plus, he had also earned the right to keep using his magical wooden bat for the rest of the season.

He slapped Coach Bergen's hand as he rounded third and ran into the crowd around home plate. Caleb's teammates spread apart so he would have a clear path to touch the base.

Once he ran across the plate, his teammates surrounded him. Caleb was crushed between all of his teammates, hugging and high-fiving each other.

He couldn't remember feeling happier or prouder on a baseball field.

"All right, everybody," Coach Bergen called. "That's enough. Let the poor kid breathe. Everybody into the dugout."

Slowly, Caleb's teammates started to head to the dugout.

Caleb scrambled to his feet. He looked around for his bat, but it wasn't anywhere to be seen.

"Hey, who picked up my bat?" Caleb yelled to the dugout. There was no response.

"Seriously, guys," he yelled. "Quit kidding around. Where is it?"

No one said a word. Finally Coach Bergen said, "It's not in here, Caleb."

Then Caleb shot a glance over at the Oilers' dugout.

The Oilers' coach, catcher, and pitcher were standing in front of the dugout. The home-plate umpire was standing with them.

That's when Caleb saw that the umpire was holding his bat. He appeared to be examining it.

Caleb jogged over to the other team's dugout. "Excuse me," he said. "Can I please have my bat back?"

The umpire didn't answer the question. "Young man, I'm going to need to talk to your coach," he said.

Caleb wasn't sure what was going on. He knew his bat was the legal size and weight. He and his father had checked the league rules before he signed up for the Spuds.

The Oilers' coach and players went into their dugout, leaving Caleb, his coach, and the umpire on the field. The umpire was still holding the bat.

"What's going on?" Coach Bergen said.

"There's an issue with the bat," the umpire said. "The other team pointed it out. Look here, on the end."

The umpire pointed to the top of the barrel of the bat.

The wood grain there was a slightly different color than the rest of the bat.

"See how it's discolored?" the umpire said. "It looks to me like this bat's been tampered with."

"Tampered with?" Caleb blurted out. He couldn't believe it. "You mean corked?"

"Look, son, I don't know what you've done to it," the umpire said.

Caleb couldn't believe his ears.

That bat had been bought right from the Original Slugger factory, when his family went on a tour during summer vacation. The bat even had an authentication stamp on the label to prove it was real.

It was one of Caleb's favorite things.

He knew for a fact that there was no way it was corked. Corking a bat made it lighter, and easier to swing. It was definitely against the rules.

Caleb hadn't done that, and there was no way the factory would have sold a corked bat.

"I haven't done anything to it," Caleb said.

"Well, I can't prove it, but it looks like someone has tampered with it," the umpire said. "I can't do anything about this game at this point, but I will tell you this: I wouldn't use it in any more league games."

The Oilers' coach, Dr. Dennis, walked over. "I'm on the league's board of directors, son," he said. "If we find out that this bat has been tampered with, you'll be suspended from the league. I wouldn't use it again if I were you."

Coach Bergen didn't say anything as he and Caleb walked back to their team's dugout.

Caleb felt terrible.

In a span of just a few minutes, he had gone from being the happiest baseball player in the world to one of the saddest.

"Coach, they've got to let me use that bat," Caleb said. "There's nothing wrong with it. I didn't do anything to it."

"I know," the coach said. "But you heard the umpire."

"But Coach," Caleb pleaded, "the bat's fine."

Coach Bergen stopped walking. He Caleb in the eye and said, "Caleb, you're using aluminum bats from now on. Period."

Chapter 4

The next night, the Spuds played
another home game, this time against
the Bucks.

Caleb brought his special bat to the
game, but he left it in his equipment bag.

Before the game, Caleb looked for an
aluminum bat that felt like his wooden
one did. He must have tried six different
bats before he found one that was close.
But it wasn't the same.

That night, Caleb struggled at the plate. He made contact with the ball every time he was up, but he didn't get any hits.

The Spuds lost, 6–5.

"Don't worry, Caleb," Coach Bergen said after the game. He could tell that Caleb was upset.

"I know you're a good hitter," the coach went on. "It's just going to take some time to adjust to the metal bats."

Caleb wasn't so sure. But over the course of the next few weeks, the aluminum bats did start to feel more comfortable.

Caleb started to get used to the feel of the aluminum bat. But he missed the satisfying weight of his magical wood bat. He also missed the way the wood bat felt in his hands.

The aluminum bat was slicker, and cold. Caleb hated it.

Caleb was not hitting the ball well. In fact, now he was one of the worst hitters on the team.

Coach Bergen dropped him lower and lower in the batting order, and finally started sitting him out of some games.

Finally, the Spuds were set for a rematch with the Oilers. Caleb couldn't wait.

Coach Bergen started him at first base, and batted him sixth in the order.

When Caleb stepped up to the plate for the first time, the Oilers' catcher was already there.

"Hey, cheater," the catcher said, smiling meanly at him.

Caleb couldn't believe what he was hearing.

"Excuse me?" he said.

"You're not such a scary hitter without your cheating bat, are you," the catcher said with a smirk.

Now Caleb was angry. He felt the blood rush to his face. He tightened his grip around the handle of his aluminum bat.

"We'll see about that," he muttered.

The Oilers' pitcher wound up and delivered a hard fastball.

Caleb reared back and swung as hard as he could. He swung so hard that he actually let out a little grunt as the bat cut through the air.

He missed the ball by a mile.

Two more pitches came. Each time, Caleb swung hard. The last time, he swung so hard he fell over.

"Strike three!" the umpire bellowed.

The catcher laughed as he tossed the ball back to the pitcher. "Nice try, cheater," he said.

Chapter 5

CALEB'S DECISION

Caleb came up to bat twice more in the game. But he struck out both times, and both times he didn't look very good doing it.

The first time, he hit a wimpy little grounder that the first baseman scooped up. He stepped on the bag easily for the out.

The second time, Caleb hit a little pop up behind home plate.

The Oilers' catcher caught it without any trouble.

By the time the last inning came around, Caleb had seen enough. He wasn't going to sit back and listen to the taunts of the Oilers' catcher anymore.

When he was on deck, he saw that he had the chance once again to decide the outcome of the game. There was no way that Caleb was going to let an aluminum bat decide this game. Not when he had a perfectly good wood bat in the dugout.

So just before it was his turn to bat, Caleb knew he had to do something. He ran into the Spuds' dugout and grabbed his wooden bat.

"Caleb, what are you doing?" one of his teammates said.

"I'm trying to win the game," Caleb said. His jaw was clenched. "This is the only way to do it."

His teammates just stared at him.

Caleb squeezed his trusty bat in his left hand and marched out to the plate.

Coach Bergen saw the wooden bat in Caleb's hands, but he didn't stop him. "I hope you know what you're doing," the coach called to Caleb.

Caleb carefully set his back foot into the batter's box and got into his batting stance. He tried to ignore the noise he heard coming from both dugouts.

The catcher watched him intently.

"I guess you decided to go back to cheating, huh?" he said, smirking at Caleb.

"Nope," Caleb replied. "I've decided to win the game."

The Spuds had a runner on third and two outs. They trailed the Oilers 7–6.

If Caleb got a hit, they could win.

Caleb dug in and stared the pitcher down.

A wide smile grew across his face.

Seeing the wood bat, the pitcher tried to throw inside pitches to Caleb. The first one nearly hit him. The second one missed the strike zone, too.

The pitcher wound up and delivered again.

Zoom!

The pitch sailed in. Caleb stepped into it and swung wildly.

Caleb was expecting to hear the crack of his bat, but instead, he heard the thud of the catcher's mitt.

He had missed.

"Strike one!" the umpire called.

"Maybe cheating won't help you this time," the catcher said, laughing. He tossed the ball back to the pitcher.

Caleb stepped out of the batter's box. He tried to calm himself down. He reminded himself that a good, solid swing beat an extra-hard swing every time.

Slow down, he thought. Swing easy. Let it happen.

The next pitch started in at Caleb's elbow. Then it broke out over the plate.

Caleb stepped into it and swung.

This time, the swing was smooth and easy. Caleb heard the *crack!* he had been hoping for.

"Great hit!" Coach Bergen cried out.

The ball headed for the hillside beyond the left-field fence.

Caleb had done it again.

Chapter 6

CHECKING IT OUT

Caleb jumped and threw his arms up into the air as he began to round the bases.

Once again, his teammates were screaming for him.

The sad Oilers players walked slowly off the field.

The group of Spuds was waiting for Caleb as he rounded third base and headed for home.

But this time, Caleb's focus was on something else.

As he ran past third base, Caleb completely missed the high five from Coach Bergen.

Caleb wasn't paying attention. He was too busy watching the Oilers' catcher walk away from home plate, holding Caleb's special wooden bat.

He ran faster toward home plate.

By the time Caleb touched home plate, the catcher had handed the bat to the Oilers' coach, Dr. Dennis.

Caleb ran over to them. Coach Bergen was right behind him.

"What's going on here, Dr. Dennis?" Coach Bergen demanded. "That's our player's bat."

"As a member of the league's board of directors, I'm going to take this bat," Dr. Dennis said. "It's a league rule that if there are questions about a piece of equipment, the league can check it out."

"There's nothing wrong with my bat," Caleb said.

"The league will decide that," Dr. Dennis said. "If the bat turns out to be fine, it will be returned to you, and you can use it."

Caleb was worried. Once the Oilers had his bat, anything could happen to it.

He worried that the Oilers players would do something to it before the league checked it out.

That would make him look bad.

Caleb tried to grab his bat, but Coach Bergen held him back.

"Let them test it, Caleb," Coach Bergen said. "Dr. Dennis is an honest man. He'll make sure that it's fine, and you'll have it back in time for the next game. We need to clear your name."

"Look, son, I won't let anything happen to it," Dr. Dennis said. "Do you have it marked somehow, so you'll know it's yours when you get it back?"

"Right there, on the end of the handle," Caleb said, pointing to the spot. "There's a big C for my name, and my uniform number, 21, inside of it. But you aren't going to break it to look inside, are you? It's really important to me."

"No," Dr. Dennis said. "We have an easy way to check this. I'll take it to my office and have it X-rayed. Then we'll know if anything is inside."

The Oilers' catcher smirked as he and his coach walked away with the bat.

"Coach, I've got a bad feeling about this," Caleb said.

Chapter 7

SOMETHING'S NOT RIGHT

Caleb wasn't sure what to expect when he showed up for his team's next game.

Would his bat be there? Would he be kicked out of the league for using an illegal bat? He didn't know.

He walked nervously into the home team's dugout. Coach Bergen was waiting there for him. The coach had a big smile on his face. Caleb had a feeling that meant the coach had good news for him.

He was right. "Well, you've got your bat back," Coach Bergen said.

He reached into his bat bag and pulled out Caleb's wooden bat. He handed it to Caleb, who immediately checked for the C-21 marking he had made on the handle. It was there.

"That's awesome," Caleb said. "What did they say?"

"Nothing," Coach Bergen said. "The bat was waiting in our dugout when I got here, with a note from Dr. Dennis. He said he'd had the bat X-rayed, and that it checked out okay."

He smiled at Caleb. "I guess that means you can use your wood bat," the coach said.

Caleb was thrilled.

As the Spuds got ready to play the Oilers again, Caleb couldn't wait for his first turn in the batter's box.

He was in a great mood. He was going to be able to use his magic bat for the rest of the season.

Caleb rushed out into the field at the top of the first inning. He got into his position at first base.

The Oilers' catcher was the first player to bat for the other team.

Caleb was stunned to see him walking to the plate carrying a wooden bat.

Caleb could tell it was the same model as his bat, but Caleb's bat was tan in color. The bat the catcher was carrying was black.

What's going on? Caleb wondered.

The Oilers' catcher swung at the first pitch and lined a base hit to center.

He rounded first base, and then jogged back to the bag.

"What's with the wood bat?" Caleb said.

"Now that I know they are legal, I thought I'd try one," the catcher said. "Pretty nice."

The Spuds struck out the next three batters to end the top of the first inning. They jogged into their dugout to get ready to hit.

Caleb was set to bat third. Coach Bergen had moved him higher in the order, since now he could use his prized wooden bat.

After the first batter of the inning reached base, Caleb was on deck. He began to warm up with his bat.

But something didn't seem right when he swung it for the first time.

The bat didn't seem to have the same weight to it. If he hadn't seen the marking on the handle, he would have thought it was a different bat.

I must be imagining things, Caleb thought.

The Spuds' second hitter popped out, so it was time for Caleb to bat. He stepped into the batter's box and stared out at the Oilers' pitcher.

Caleb swung his bat lightly back and forth, readying himself for the pitch. The bat still seemed strange, but he ignored it.

The pitcher wound up and delivered. Caleb saw the ball clearly the whole way. It was right in his hitting zone.

Caleb's back leg drove forward and his hips turned.

The bat powered through the zone.

But when the bat met the ball, all Caleb heard was a soft thud.

The ball glanced off toward the first base side. It was foul. Caleb had just missed it.

He wasn't worried about the foul ball. After all, that happened all the time. But not only did his bat feel weird, it suddenly sounded weird too.

Something was different.

Caleb tried to ignore it.

The pitcher was ready to deliver again.

Once again, the pitch was perfect for Caleb. This time, he decided, he would not miss it.

Caleb pounced on the pitch and met it with the meat of his bat.

Crackle!

It was not the noise Caleb wanted to hear.

Instead of the crack of a solid hit, Caleb heard the sound of his prized bat shattering into a million pieces.

As the barrel of the bat split in half the long way, something else popped out. Caleb watched in amazement as bits of cork flew in all directions.

Chapter 8

The umpire jumped out from behind home plate. He immediately picked up the two big pieces of the bat's barrel.

Coaches from both teams ran to the scene.

Caleb stood there, shocked. He didn't know what to do next.

When he looked at the inside of the bat, he could see that a hole had been drilled into it.

The hole had been filled with pieces of cork, and then sealed at the top.

Without a word, the umpire made a quick motion with his hand, throwing Caleb out of the game.

Caleb glanced around the field. All the Oilers players were laughing.

The catcher was laughing really hard. "I knew he was a cheater!" he said.

There was nothing Caleb could do. He had used an illegal bat. There was no way to argue that point. But he knew it wasn't really his bat. He just didn't have a way to prove it.

Caleb was speechless. The umpire had handed the bat pieces to Coach Bergen, who handed them to Caleb. He eyed them carefully.

"Here's what's left of your bat, Caleb," Coach Bergen said. "I guess Dr. Dennis's X-ray machine was broken. I can't believe what just happened out there. That's not like you at all. I've never known you to be a cheater."

Then Caleb realized something. Before Coach Bergen could finish, Caleb interrupted. "Coach, it's not mine!" he said.

"You need to leave the field, young man," the umpire said.

"Listen, Caleb, I don't want to hear any excuses," Coach Bergen said.

"But, Coach, this isn't my bat!" Caleb yelled.

Coach Bergen looked angry. "Caleb, you know it's your bat," he said. "It has the marking you put on the handle."

He started to walk away.

"Yeah, but it doesn't have the factory stamp," Caleb said.

Coach Bergen turned around.

Caleb showed him the label on the broken bat. It had the same Original Slugger logo, but it didn't have the same factory authentication stamp that Caleb's bat had.

It wasn't a bat straight from the factory. It had been purchased in a sporting goods store.

"Somebody replaced my bat with this one," Caleb said.

By then, Dr. Dennis had reached them. Coach Bergen was looking for answers. "Dr. Dennis, what happened to Caleb's bat?" the coach asked.

"I took it to my office and had it X-rayed, and it checked out fine," Dr. Dennis said. "Solid wood. So I sent it back to you guys."

"Well, it looks like we ended up with a different bat," Coach Bergen said. "Is it possible there was some kind of mistake?"

Dr. Dennis looked puzzled. "I don't see how," he said. "I handed the bat to Davey myself, and asked him to put it in your dugout with the note from me."

"Davey?" Caleb blurted out. "Isn't he your catcher?"

Caleb shot a glance over at the Oilers' catcher, who looked away.

"Now hold on a minute," Dr. Dennis said. "You're not suggesting that Davey had anything to do with this, are you?"

The umpire interrupted. "Gentlemen, we have to sort this out later," he said. "We have a game to play. The hitter is out of the game."

Caleb was walking away when it hit him. He turned and sprinted for the Oilers' dugout.

He reached the bat rack and snatched the catcher's black wooden bat off it. He turned it over and looked at the label.

There, just as he suspected, was the authentication stamp from the Original Slugger factory.

"This is my bat! He painted it black!" Caleb said.

Dr. Dennis looked at Davey.

Davey stared at the ground.

"Davey, take your catcher's gear off," Dr. Dennis said. "As a member of the board of directors, I can't let you continue to play."

Davey slowly took off the gear and left the field.

Caleb watched the rest of the game from the bleachers. But he knew that from now on, finally, he could play the game he loved, using the bat he loved.

About the Author

Bob Temple lives in Rosemount, Minnesota, with his wife and three children. He has written more than thirty books for children. Over the years, he has coached more than twenty kids' soccer, basketball, and baseball teams. He also loves visiting classrooms to talk about his writing.

About the Illustrator

When Sean Tiffany was growing up, he lived on a small island off the coast of Maine. Every day, from sixth grade until he graduated from high school, he had to take a boat to get to school. When Sean isn't working on his art, he works on a multimedia project called "OilCan Drive," which combines music and art. He has a pet cactus named Jim.

Glossary

aluminum (uh-LOO-mih-nuhm)—a light, silver-colored metal

authentication (aw-then-tih-KAY-shuhn)—proving that something is real

barrel (BARE-uhl)—the thick part of a bat

corked (KORKD)—if a bat is corked, it has been filled with cork to make it lighter

discolored (diss-KUHL-urd)—stained or changed in color

legal (LEE-guhl)—allowed. Illegal is the opposite of legal and means not allowed.

on deck (ON DEK)—if a player is on deck, he or she will bat next

outcome (OUT-kuhm)—a result

tamper (TAM-pur)—to interfere with something so that it is damaged or broken

umpire (UHM-pire)—the official who rules on plays

Wood or Aluminum?

It used to be that all baseball bats were made out of wood.

Today, only professional baseball players are required to use wood bats. At all other levels, including college and high school baseball, players can use aluminum bats or bats made of other materials.

Youth baseball organizations started using aluminum bats many years ago, mainly because they lasted longer.

Youth sports organizations have limited budgets, and having to replace broken wood bats was expensive. While an aluminum bat might be more expensive at first, they almost never break, so they can last for many years.

Recently, safety organizations have raised concerns about aluminum bats.

You Decide!

Because a baseball "jumps" off of an aluminum bat faster than off a wooden one, the ball heads out faster toward the fielders.

This is particularly dangerous for the pitcher. The pitcher is the closest player to home plate, and can often be off-balance after delivering a pitch. Some pitchers have been seriously injured by fast line drives that come directly back at them off of aluminum bats.

Of course, there is no way to completely avoid the dangers of playing any sport. But some youth organizations are discussing returning to the use of wooden bats for these safety reasons.

Plus, using a wood bat makes you just like a big leaguer!

Discussion Questions

1. Why do you think Davey tampered with Caleb's bat?

2. The Oilers and Spuds were rival teams. Do any of your sports teams have rivals like that? Talk about rivalry. What is your experience with it? What is it like to compete against a rival? Do you think it is good or bad to have a rival?

3. Why did Caleb's coach want him to use an aluminum bat? Why did Caleb want to use a wood bat? Talk about both sides of the problem.

Writing Prompts

1. Sometimes it's interesting to think about a story from another person's point of view. Try writing chapter 8 from Davey's point of view. What does he think about? What does he see? How does it feel to him?

2. Caleb bought his bat on a summer trip. Have you ever taken a memorable vacation? Describe it. If you haven't, describe a vacation you'd like to take!

3. When the bat Caleb used breaks open and cork pops out, Caleb is thrown out of the game. Have you ever been accused of something that wasn't your fault? Write about the experience.

OTHER BOOKS

JAKE MADDOX

QUARTERBACK SNEAK

STONE ARCH *Realistic Fiction*

Anton loves playing football until Malik, the talented quarterback, starts acting strange. Instead of working with the team, Malik is just showing off. Anton has to fix the problem fast, before the quarterback ruins everything!

BY JAKE MADDOX

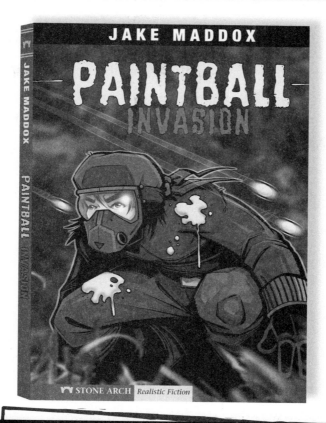

JAKE MADDOX

PAINTBALL INVASION

STONE ARCH *Realistic Fiction*

Josh and Chad have been using the same place as a paintball field forever. But now, someone's attacking them! Who's out to stop their paintballing fun? It's going to take all the skills they have to stop the sabotage.

Internet Sites

Do you want to know more about subjects related to this book? Or are you interested in learning about other topics? Then check out FactHound, a fun, easy way to find Internet sites.

Our investigative staff has already sniffed out great sites for you!

Here's how to use FactHound:

1. Visit *www.facthound.com*

2. Select your grade level.

3. To learn more about subjects related to this book, type in the book's ISBN number: **9781434204653**.

4. Click the **Fetch It** button.

FactHound will fetch the best Internet sites for you!